1944
MOLLY'S SURPRISE

A Christmas Story

By VALERIE TRIPP

ILLUSTRATIONS NICK BACKES

VIGNETTES KEITH SKEEN, RENÉE GRAEF

AmericanGirl ™

Printed in the United States of America.
01 02 03 04 05 06 07 08 QWT 41 40 39 38 37 36 35

The American Girls Collection®, Molly®, Molly McIntire®, and American Girl®
are trademarks of Pleasant Company.

PICTURE CREDITS
The following individuals and organizations have generously given
permission to reprint images contained in "Looking Back": pp. 60-61—Reprinted from *House
Beautiful,* © December 1942, The Hearst Corporation. All rights reserved. Eugene Hutchinson,
photographer; reprinted from *House Beautiful,* © December 1942, The Hearst Corporation. All
rights reserved. Luis Lemus, photographer; State Historical Society of Wisconsin WHi(x3)21422;
State Historical Society of Wisconsin WHi(x3)42010; pp. 62-63—Jane & Michael Stern, *Square
Meals,* Alfred A. Knopf, New York, © 1984; reprinted from *House Beautiful,* © December 1942, The
Hearst Corporation. All rights reserved; reprinted from *House Beautiful,* © December 1942, The
Hearst Corporation. All rights reserved. Robert Keene Studios, photographer; pp. 64-65—Sears,
Roebuck & Co.; courtesy of the Hallmark Archives, Hallmark Cards, Inc.; Library of Congress.

Edited by Jeanne Thieme
Designed by Myland McRevey and Ingrid Slamer
Cover Background by John Pugh

Library of Congress Cataloging-in-Publication Data

Tripp, Valerie, 1951-
Molly's surprise: a Christmas story
by Valerie Tripp; illustrations, Nick Backes; vignettes, Keith Skeen, Renée Graef.

p.cm.—(The American girls collection)
Summary: Even though he is away serving in an English hospital during
World War II, Molly's father finds a way to make the family Christmas very special.
[1. Christmas—Fiction. 2. Family life—Fiction. 3. World War, 1939-1945—
United States—Fiction.]
I. Backes, Nick, ill. II. Title. III. Series.
PZ7.T7363Mp 1990 [Fic]—dc19 89-3887
ISBN 0-937295-87-6
ISBN 0-937295-25-6 (pbk.)

TO MICHAEL

TABLE OF CONTENTS

MOLLY'S FAMILY

MOLLY
A nine-year-old who is growing up on the home front in America during World War Two.

DAD
Molly's father, a doctor who is somewhere in England, taking care of wounded soldiers.

MOM
Molly's mother, who holds the family together while Dad is away.

JILL
Molly's fourteen-year-old sister, who is always trying to act grown-up.

RICKY
*Molly's twelve-year-old
brother—a big pest.*

BRAD
*Molly's five-year-old
brother—a little pest.*

MRS. GILFORD
*The housekeeper, who
rules the roost when
Mom is at work.*

LINDA
*One of Molly's best
friends, a practical
schemer.*

SUSAN
*Molly's other best
friend, a cheerful
dreamer.*

CHAPTER One

A DIFFERENT CHRISTMAS

December 21

Dear Dad,

Merry Christmas! How are you? I am fine except I wish you could somehow magically be home for Christmas. Do you have a Christmas tree in the hospital? I hope so. Gram and Granpa are bringing our Christmas tree tomorrow. I hope it's a big one! Right now, Mom is making a wreath for the front door and Ricky and Brad are listening to the radio. Jill is knitting. I hope you got the presents we sent you. We haven't gotten any presents from you yet. Probably they will come soon. XOXOXOX

"Hey, I don't think you should write that."

Molly stopped making X's and O's on her letter and turned around. Jill was behind her, lounging sideways across Dad's chair, her legs dangling over one arm. She was reading the letter over Molly's shoulder.

"Write what?" asked Molly.

"That part about how we haven't gotten any presents from him."

"Why not?"

Jill swung her legs up and down. "Because," she said in a very patient voice, "Christmas is only four days away. By the time Dad gets that letter, Christmas will be over. If he didn't send us any presents—"

"But he did! I'm sure he did," said Molly. "Dad would never forget to send us Christmas presents."

Jill continued. "If he *didn't* send us any presents, he'll feel bad when he gets your letter. But by then it will be too late for him to do anything about it. And if he did send us presents, he'll feel bad because we never got them." She turned to her mother. "Don't you think I'm right, Mom?"

Mrs. McIntire was tying a bright red bow on

*"Dad would never forget to
send us Christmas presents," Molly said.*

the pine wreath. "I think it is Molly's letter and she should write whatever she wants to write."

Jill shrugged. She started to knit again.

Brad piped up. "Maybe Dad's present was on a plane that got shot down by the Germans and drowned in the ocean."

"That's possible," said Ricky. Ricky considered himself an expert on fighter planes. "Those guys try to shoot down anything that flies." He took aim with an imaginary machine gun and fired at an imaginary plane. "POW! POW! POW!"

Brad looked up at his mother. "Will the Germans shoot down Santa's sleigh?"

"Of course not!" said Mrs. McIntire. She rumpled Brad's hair. "I'm sure Santa will get here safe and sound."

"I hope so," said Brad. "And I sure hope he brings me a soldier's hat and a real canteen."

"We'll just have to wait and see what Santa brings," said Mrs. McIntire. She stood up and took Brad's hand. "Come on. You can help me hang the wreath on the door. Then it's time for bed. Tomorrow is a big day. Gram and Granpa are going to bring us our Christmas tree."

As they walked into the hall together, Mrs. McIntire began, "'Twas the night before . . ."

"Christmas!" Brad ended.

"And all through the . . ."

"House!"

"Not a creature was . . ."

"Stirring!"

"Not even a . . ."

"Mouse!"

When they were gone, Jill stopped knitting. "Boy, I feel sorry for Brad," she said.

"Why?" asked Molly.

"For lots of reasons," said Jill. She tapped the palm of her hand with a knitting needle as she listed each reason. "First of all, Dad's gone. It hardly seems like Christmas without Dad here. And on top of that, there are no presents from him."

"Yet," corrected Molly. "No presents from Dad *yet*."

Jill ignored the interruption. "Then there's this Santa Claus business. Brad will be so disappointed when all he gets from Santa are boring presents like socks and handkerchiefs. It's not so bad for us.

We're old enough not to mind. But he's still just a little kid. He wants that hat and canteen so badly. He won't understand why he can't have them." Jill stabbed her knitting needle into the ball of yarn.

"You mean he's not going to get them?" asked Molly.

Ricky sat up. "Real soldiers need hats and canteens," he said. "They don't have any to spare."

Molly had an uncomfortable feeling that Jill and Ricky were right.

"Besides," said Jill, "you know how Mom believes it's not patriotic to spend money on unnecessary things like toys. I'm sure all our presents this year will be homemade or hand-me-downs." She stretched and yawned. "I'm just glad there's nothing I really, really want, so I won't be disappointed."

"But that's not true," said Molly. "You really, really want a skating hat like the one you're making for Dolores, don't you?"

"Sure, I do," said Jill. "So I've been saving my baby-sitting money to buy one for myself. I know that's the only way I'll get it. It's childish to expect surprises this Christmas."

"But remember what Dad used to say?" said Molly. "There are *always* surprises at Christmas."

"This Christmas is different," said Jill. "This is wartime. There just won't be any wonderful surprises this year. We have to be realistic."

"Realistic" was one of Jill's new words. It always sounded gloomy to Molly. Being realistic meant expecting things to be ordinary and dull. Molly did not want to feel that way about Christmas. And suddenly, she did not want to be part of this conversation anymore.

She stood up and put her letter to Dad in her pocket. "Well, I think I'm going to bed now." She hurried out of the room before Jill could say anything else realistic, and ran up the stairs two at a time.

Molly closed the door to her room. She sat on the window seat and looked out at the night. It was very dark. The black sky seemed to push up against her window. There were no stars to pin it back where it belonged. Molly hugged her knees to her chest and thought about what Jill had said.

She knew Jill was right about one thing at least. It would be a simple Christmas. She should expect practical presents—things she really needed rather than things she dreamed about.

Molly hugged her knees tighter. She didn't *need* the present she wanted more than anything else: a doll. Not a baby doll, but a doll she could have adventures with. Jill would say it was childish and unpatriotic to want something as unnecessary as a doll. And Molly knew it was certainly unrealistic to hope for a doll. But she couldn't help it. She couldn't stop hoping that by some magic, some

8

Christmas magic, a new doll would be under the tree for her on Christmas morning. She couldn't stop hoping that the magic would bring something from Dad, too.

Because Dad loved Christmas. It was his favorite time of year. Right after Thanksgiving he would begin singing Christmas carols. Sometimes he would change the words to make Molly laugh. He would sing:

> "Deck the halls with boughs of holly,
> Fa-la-la-la-la, la-la-la-la.
> 'Tis the season to be Molly,
> Fa-la-la-la-la, la-la-la-la!"

Every year Dad made funny presents, too, and wrapped them in green tissue paper. No one could wait to open his surprises on Christmas morning. One year he made everyone—even Mom—a kite. The next year everyone got a yo-yo. Molly took her letter to Dad out of her pocket. Should she cross out the part about the presents? Maybe this year Dad was too busy to think of Christmas surprises. Things were probably very realistic where Dad was, in the middle of fighting. Molly sighed.

Just then there was a knock on the door and Molly's mother poked her head in. Her hand was covering her eyes. "May I come in? Or is this Santa's workshop? I don't want to see any presents before I'm supposed to."

Molly smiled. "It's okay, Mom. All my presents are already wrapped and hidden away."

Mom sat down on the window seat. "You're just like your father. His presents are always wrapped and ready before anyone else's."

"Not this year," said Molly. "I'm beginning to think maybe there won't be any presents from Dad this year. Maybe it's wrong to keep hoping."

"Now, Molly. Don't tell me you've given up on Dad."

"I don't know," said Molly slowly. "I want to think that a present will come. There is still enough time before Christmas. But . . ." Molly stopped. She looked down at her letter to Dad. The Christmas

 tree she had drawn was a little cock-eyed. "But Jill says we have to be realistic. She says the war has made this Christmas different."

Mrs. McIntire reached over and

smoothed Molly's bangs. "This Christmas *will* be different, Molly. Jill is right. We do have to be realistic about some things. We can't pretend there's no war. We can't pretend Dad is home. We can't ignore what's real."

"But I want Christmas to be special," said Molly. "I want Christmas to be full of surprises the way it is when Dad is home."

"So do I," said her mother. "And this Christmas can be special, but it will be up to us to make it special. If Dad can't be here to make our surprises for us, we'll just have to make them for ourselves." She grinned at Molly. "I think everyone in the McIntire family is pretty good at making surprises. I know I have a few surprises up my sleeve, and I bet you do, too." She leaned over and gave Molly a quick kiss on the forehead. "But it's never wrong to keep hoping for good things to happen, Molly, especially at Christmas time. That's what Christmas is all about—hope." As she turned to close the door behind her, she said, "Good night, dear. Don't forget to brush your teeth before you go to bed."

"Good night, Mom," said Molly. She leaned her forehead against the cool windowpane. There were no stars to wish on. So she closed her eyes and made her wish deep inside herself. "I hope Dad's presents come. And I hope there will be lots of wonderful surprises this Christmas."

CHAPTER TWO

MAKING SURPRISES

Molly's nose was tickled awake by a spicy smell. She sat up and took a deep breath. *Mmmm, cinnamon,* she thought. *Mom must be making sticky buns as a surprise for breakfast.* Molly grinned. She remembered what Mom had said the night before about making their own surprises. It looked—or rather, it smelled—as if Mom's surprises were already off to a delicious start.

Molly rolled out of bed and pulled on old corduroys and a flannel shirt. They had a nice, soft, easy, vacation-y feeling. In them, Molly was ready for something unusual to happen. *If only I had a doll,* she thought as she pulled on a pair of thick socks.

This is just the kind of day when we would have an adventure together. Maybe we'd pretend to be ambulance drivers, or scientists cooking up some interesting concoction. . . .

Molly hurried into her shoes. The only concoction that interested her right now was being cooked up downstairs in the kitchen. She'd better hurry down before Ricky ate up all the sticky buns.

She bounced down the stairs to the kitchen. But Ricky wasn't there. "Good morning, Mom," said Molly. "Where's Ricky?"

"He's already in the living room," said Mrs. McIntire. "He's moving furniture to make room for the Christmas tree."

Just as Molly bit into the warm, sweet bun, Ricky appeared at her elbow. "Hurry up and eat that," he said in a businesslike voice. "I need you to help me bring up the ornaments."

Molly's mouth was too full to answer, so she nodded her head eagerly. Ricky waited impatiently as she chewed and swallowed, gulped some milk, and wiped her sticky fingers. "Let's go," he commanded.

Molly followed Ricky down the dark steep steps

to the cellar. There was only one light behind them, a bare bulb hanging at the top of the stairs. Their shadows danced before them like cheerful ghosts. They seemed to say, "Here you are at last! We've been waiting all year for you to come down and open this closet! Now the fun can begin!"

Molly jumped ahead of Ricky and pulled open the closet door. Every Christmas she could remember had begun the same way. Dad would open this door—the door to the Christmas closet—and say, "Ho, ho, ho! What have we here?"

The closet was full of Christmas. It smelled of dried pine needles, mothballs, crushed peppermint candy canes, and bayberry-scented candles. Bags overflowed with curlicued ribbons, paper chains, rolls of wrapping paper, and shiny strands of tinsel. Boxes of Christmas tree ornaments were piled in shaky stacks. They were waiting to be carried upstairs and dusted off, so they could shine in the light and work their Christmas magic again. Molly was glad to see them. She scooped up an armload and held the boxes steady with her chin.

Ricky pulled a string of Christmas tree lights off the shelf. "I'll take care of these this year," he said.

"I'll take care of these this year,"
Ricky said.

Molly was doubtful. No one but Dad had ever handled the lights before. It was a big job. The tangled string of lights looked like a thorny vine. "Do you think you can do it?" she asked. "Even Dad has trouble. . . ."

"Don't worry, fuss-budget. I can figure these out," Ricky said. He slung the loop of lights over his shoulder and marched up the stairs.

Molly climbed the stairs behind him. With every step she took, a bell jingled in one of the boxes she carried. "Ho, ho, ho!" she said as she jiggled the box to make the bell ring louder. "Here comes Christmas!"

Brad ran to meet her at the top of the stairs. "Oh! Let me see!" he cried. "Where's my stocking?" Molly lowered her pile of boxes to the floor and knelt to open them.

"Hey, look!" Brad held up a battered star cut out of cardboard and covered with wrinkled tinfoil. "Here's the star I made last year."

Jill sat at the kitchen table calmly eating a sticky bun with a fork. She glanced down at the boxes scattered on the floor. "Oh, *honestly*," she said with a scowl. "Did you have to haul all that stuff out of the basement?"

Molly looked up. "But these are the Christmas tree ornaments. We need them."

Jill raised her eyebrows, then turned back to her sticky bun. "They're so . . . junky. I think this year we should use only store-bought balls, none of those homemade ornaments or messy paper chains."

No one said anything.

Jill touched her lips with her napkin. "And I think we should use only blue and red balls and blue and red lights. It will look patriotic."

Molly thought that was a terrible idea. "But we don't have very many blue and red balls," she said.

"We don't need many," said Jill. "We usually put too much junk on the tree anyway. It will look more elegant with just a few balls."

Brad looked down at his tinfoil star.

"I don't want the tree to look *elegant*," said Molly. "I want it to look—"

"Just like last year," interrupted Jill. "I know. You want everything to be just like last year. And I

18

keep telling you it just can't be."

Ricky put the string of lights on the table. "What do you think, Mom?" he asked.

Mrs. McIntire put her hands in the pockets of her apron. "Well, I think it would be nice to have an elegant, patriotic tree. But I know I would miss all the old ornaments. They're like old friends." She thought for a moment. "How about this? I saw a picture in a magazine of a Christmas tree with a flag on top instead of an angel or a star. It looked very patriotic. What if we used all of our old ornaments but put a flag at the top of our tree?"

"That would be good!" said Brad.

Molly looked at Jill. "What do you think, Jill?"

Jill shrugged. "Frankly, I don't really care. It was just a suggestion." She stepped over the boxes of ornaments and walked to the sink to wash her plate.

"Well!" said Mom in a cheerful voice. "That's settled! Brad and I are going downtown today anyway. We'll just add a flag to our shopping list."

Right after breakfast, Mom and Brad got ready to go out. Brad's pockets were so full of pennies he'd saved for buying presents that he clanked when he walked. "You sound like a walking piggy bank," said Jill.

As Mrs. McIntire put on her coat, she said, "We'll have lunch in town. But we'll be back before Gram and Granpa get here with the Christmas tree."

No sooner had Mom and Brad disappeared from sight than the phone rang. Ricky was on his hands and knees trying to untangle a string of lights stretched across the living room. "It's probably for you, Jill," he said. "It almost always is."

Jill picked up the telephone. "Hello? Oh, hello, Grammy!" she said with a smile. "No, Mom's not here. She and Brad are shopping."

As Ricky and Molly watched, Jill's smile sank into a worried frown. "Oh," she said. "Oh, that's too bad. Can't you get it fixed? Oh." She turned away so they could only see her back. "Yes, I'll tell Mom. Well, we'll . . . we'll certainly miss you. No,

no presents have come from Dad yet. I'll tell Mom
to call if a box arrives. Well, we're sorry, too. Say
hello to Granpa for us. Good-bye." She hung up.

"What happened?" asked Molly. "What's the
matter?"

Jill turned around. "They can't come," she
stated.

"What?" gasped Ricky and Molly together.

"Grammy says they had a flat tire. Their spare
tire is too old to use on such a long trip. So
they'll have to wait and get the other
tire patched. No one can do it until

21

after the weekend. So," she repeated grimly, "they can't come."

"Oh, no!" wailed Molly. She sat down on the floor next to a box of ornaments.

"Oh, boy. What a Christmas!" said Ricky glumly. "First no Dad. Now no Gram and Granpa."

"And no *tree*," said Molly. "No Christmas tree from Gram and Granpa's farm."

"Well, what do we need a tree for anyway?" asked Ricky. He kicked away a string of lights with his foot. "We don't have any presents from Dad to put under it."

"We have our presents for each other," Molly said weakly.

"Big deal," said Ricky.

Molly began to feel as gloomy as she had the night before. "I wish Mom were here," she said.

"Mom couldn't do anything about it," said Ricky. "Let's face it. This Christmas is ruined. No one can do anything about it."

Molly thought about what Mom had told her last night. "Mom says we have to rely on ourselves this Christmas. She says *we* have to make Christmas special this year."

"What are we supposed to do?" asked Ricky. "Make a Christmas tree?"

Jill had been very quiet, but now she said, "We could buy a tree. We could do that ourselves."

"How?" said Ricky. "I only have twenty-five cents left."

"I have money," said Jill.

"But that's your baby-sitting money," said Molly. "I thought you were saving that for—"

"A tree is more important," Jill interrupted. "Come on. Let's hurry. Let's get the tree before Mom and Brad get home."

"Wait a minute," said Molly. She ran upstairs, rummaged in the closet, then ran down-stairs again. "Here," she panted. She showed Jill a lumpy package wrapped in red paper. "This is—this *was* my Christmas present for Brad. It's fifty pennies. We may need it."

Jill nodded briskly. "Good," she said. "Now we have plenty."

Jill led the way. Molly and Ricky hurried to catch up. "But where will we get a tree?" asked Ricky as he stumbled along, trying to button up his jacket.

"Boy Scouts are selling trees at the school," said Jill. "Hurry up."

The Boy Scouts had created a small forest of pines in a corner of the school playground. Molly, Jill, and Ricky walked through it slowly, examining each tree carefully. Finally, Jill stopped. "This is it," she said.

Molly looked at the tree. It was tall and skinny. There were so many gaps between branches, it looked like a comb with most of its teeth missing. "This one?" she asked. "But—"

Ricky jabbed her with his elbow. He pointed to the price tag. Suddenly, Molly understood. This was the only tree they could afford to buy.

Jill gave all of her baby-sitting money to the Boy Scout in charge. Ricky handed him his twenty-five cents. Molly poured fifty pennies into the Boy Scout's hands. They each grabbed on to the trunk of the tree and headed home.

"Well, at least it's not heavy," said Ricky.

Molly looked at the tree. It was scrawny. But it had the sharp pine scent that meant Christmas. Molly broke off a needle and bit it. A bitter piney tang filled her mouth. "Let's decorate the tree before

24

"This is it," Jill said.

Mom and Brad get home," she said. "That way it will be a great surprise for them."

Jill shook her head. "You and your surprises," she said. But Molly could tell Jill was excited, too, because she began to walk a little faster. The tree bounced with every step.

This tree is going to be okay, Molly thought as they hurried home in the pale December sunshine. *Mom and Brad will be so surprised. And we did it all by ourselves.* Molly grinned. *I guess Mom was right. All the McIntires are pretty good at surprises.*

It was dark before dinnertime. Molly and Jill were lying on the living room floor, gazing up through the branches of the decorated Christmas tree. Once it had been decorated, the tree did not look scrawny at all. In fact, Molly thought it looked beautiful.

"Jill, do you mind that we put all the old

ornaments on the tree?" she asked. "Are you disappointed that it's not elegant?"

"No," said Jill. "This tree *needed* all the ornaments. Besides, I didn't really like that idea of only red and blue balls. I just thought it might be better if the tree looked different this year." She sighed. "See, when everything looks the same as last year, it just makes me miss Dad even more. Everything is the same except for one big, horrible difference—Dad isn't here."

"Oh," said Molly. "I never thought of it that way." She looked up at the colored lights wound around the tree. They looked like shining jewels on the green branches. "Well, I think this is the most beautiful Christmas tree we've ever had."

Jill smiled. "You say that every year."

"I know," said Molly. "But this year it's true. Even Mom said so."

Molly and Jill were happily quiet. They were both thinking of when Mom and Brad had come home to the glittering tree. Molly had never seen her mother so completely surprised. She shivered with pleasure when she recalled Mom's pleased, proud face.

"You know what, Jill? I'm beginning to think that making surprises for other people is more fun than getting surprises yourself."

"Mmmm," said Jill.

Molly couldn't tell if Jill was listening or not, but she went on. "I mean, it will still be great to get Dad's surprises, of course."

Jill tapped one of the dangling balls so that it swung back and forth like the pendulum of a clock. "How come you're still so sure we'll get presents from Dad?" she asked.

Molly was silent for a moment. Should she say out loud the worry she had been carrying around for days? She took a deep breath. "Oh, Jill," Molly said, "I have to keep thinking a package will come because if it doesn't I'm scared it means . . ." She stopped.

Jill rolled onto her side and propped her head on her hand. "If nothing comes, it means Dad may be hurt or sick or lost. It means maybe he *couldn't* send any presents."

Molly nodded. It was kind of a relief to know

that Jill shared the same heavy worry.

"It's not really the presents I care about," said Molly. "I just hope a box or something—even a card or a letter—will come so we'll know Dad is okay."

"I know what you mean," said Jill. "I'm worried about exactly the same thing. I bet Mom and Ricky are, too."

Molly looked up through the tangle of branches. Brad's tinfoil star was near the top of the tree, next to a yellow light. *Please let Dad be okay*, Molly wished. The tinfoil star seemed to twinkle just like a real star that was trying to reassure her. Molly wondered if Jill saw it, too.

KEEPING SECRETS

Something wonderful had happened. Molly knew it the minute she woke up. Her room was full of sunshine. Light shimmered and danced on the walls. Molly pushed back the covers and hurried out of bed. The floor was cold to her bare feet, so she hopped from rug to rug as if they were stepping-stones across an icy stream. She looked out the window. SNOW. Beautiful, perfect, bright white snow all over everything, as thick as icing on a cake.

Oh, boy, snow! thought Molly. She couldn't wait to get outside into all that deep, clean whiteness.

Molly didn't stop to get dressed. With her socks

and shoes in hand, she rushed across the hall and burst into Jill's room. Jill was snuggled so deep under the covers that only the top of her head showed.  Her hair was bobby-pinned in rows of tight curls so that her head looked like a prickly pineapple resting on the pillow.

Molly shook her shoulder. "Jill!" she whispered urgently. "Wake up!"

Jill rolled over and opened one eye. "What?"

"Come on. Get up. It *snowed*." Molly wobbled on one foot, pulling a sock on the other foot as she talked.

"Ohhhhh," Jill moaned. "Go away."

"But Jill," said Molly, "it's the first snow of the winter. Don't you want to go out and—"

"No!" Jill snapped. "I want to sleep. I can't believe you woke me up just because of some stupid snow. Now go away." She pulled the covers over her head.

Molly backed out of Jill's room and closed the door. Last year, Jill woke Molly up the first time it snowed. She was just as excited as Molly was. They made outlines of angels all over the driveway by

 lying on their backs in the snow and moving their arms up and down. Molly sighed. She should have realized Jill wouldn't care about the snow this year. Now that Jill was fourteen, she didn't get excited about anything that was fun anymore. She was *realistic.*

Molly tiptoed downstairs to the kitchen. She pulled on her snow jacket, boots, hat, and mittens and went outside. The whole world was blue sky and white snow. It was as if Molly had stepped out of her same old back door into an enchanted land no one had ever seen or touched before. It was hers alone. Yesterday the trees were sad, scrawny black skeletons. Today their branches were soft white arms opened wide, outstretched to welcome the snow. Everything was smoothed and softened by the sparkling blanket of white.

With a wild whoop, Molly took a flying leap off the stairs into a drift of snow. It was like jumping into a cloud. A car made its way slowly down the street, its tire chains jingling like bells on a sleigh.

The snow came to the top of Molly's boots. She scooped up a handful to lick. *Snow for Christmas,*

she thought. *It's perfect. It's a great big giant
Christmas surprise. Now the whole entire world will
be ready for Christmas.* She wondered what Dad's
Christmas would be like in England. Maybe the
fighting would stop for a while. The doctors and
nurses in the hospital might have a Christmas
party. Would they sing Christmas carols and give
each other presents?

Molly wished she were old enough to be a
Red Cross nurse. Then she could go to England
and work in the hospital with Dad. She'd wear a
uniform as white as this morning's snow and a cap

with a red cross on it. "Nurse McIntire," that's
what the soldiers would call her. She'd ride in the
ambulance out to the battlefields and rescue the
poor wounded soldiers while guns fired all around
her. Nothing would scare her. Nothing would stop
her, not blizzards, or bombs, or—WHACK! Something cold and wet hit Molly on the leg. It was a
snowball!

"Bombs away!" yelled Ricky from his bedroom
window. He launched another snowball at Molly.

"Cut it out," Molly laughed. She threw a
handful of snow up at him. Ricky had made a

stockpile of balls from the snow around
his windows. Molly ran and dodged
as he pelted her with snowball after
snowball.

Ricky imitated the deep voice radio announcers
used when they described American airplanes
bombing the enemy: "Our brave fliers! Bombers who
can hit (Smack!) any target with deadly accuracy.
(Whack!) Nothing can stop these Flying Fortresses
from (Got ya!) delivering their tons and tons of
bombs. (Bam!)"

Suddenly Jill appeared on the back steps.

"Richard Culver McIntire!" she said in her bossiest voice. "Close that window immediately. You'll freeze the entire house."

Ricky chucked his last snowball at Jill and then vanished. Molly looked at her sister. "I thought you wanted to sleep."

Jill grinned back and shrugged. "I figured I was already awake. I might as well come out."

"Let's go make angels in the front yard," said Molly.

"Okay," said Jill. Her cheeks were already as red as Christmas bows.

Molly made a chain of neat bootprints in a single line around the corner of the house. Jill stepped in the prints Molly made. They always liked to leave the snow as pure and unmarked as possible.

"Our house looks as perfect as an old-fashioned Christmas card, doesn't it?" Molly sighed as she looked up at Mom's wreath on the front door. Suddenly, she stopped walking. What was that lump on the front porch, right under the wreath? She began to run, slipping and sliding across the smooth white yard, stumbling up the steps to the front door. She dropped to her knees on the top step.

"Jill!" she said. "Come quick!" She began digging wildly at the lump, sending the snow whirling in a small blizzard.

"What is it?" asked Jill. Then she saw it, too— a box as big as a suitcase, half buried in the snow.

Molly brushed the snow off the top of the box. Jill read the label:

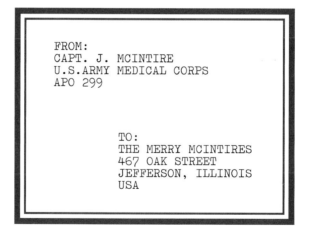

```
FROM:
CAPT. J. MCINTIRE
U.S.ARMY MEDICAL CORPS
APO 299



       TO:
       THE MERRY MCINTIRES
       467 OAK STREET
       JEFFERSON, ILLINOIS
       USA
```

"It's from Dad! It's from Dad!" said Molly. She felt happiness exploding inside her like fireworks.

She hugged the box as if it were her father. "Come on! Let's dig it out and go show everybody. Wait until they see!"

Jill was too happy to talk. She sat right down on the steps and helped Molly clear the snow away from the box. The brown paper was torn and ragged, spotted with stamps and stickers.

Molly dug all the snow away from one end of the box. There, in big letters, was a message. It said:

KEEP HIDDEN UNTIL CHRISTMAS DAY!

It was Dad's handwriting. Molly would know it anywhere. It was as familiar as his face. Molly could almost hear her father's voice saying those words. The voice would be full of fun, but serious, too.

"Jill, look at this." Molly pointed to the words.

Jill read the message. "Keep hidden . . ." she whispered.

"Dad wants us to hide the box until Christmas. That's two days away," said Molly.

Jill frowned. "I don't know if we *should* hide it. I'm so glad it's here, because it means Dad is okay.

"Where should we put it?" asked Jill.
"We can't take it into the house."

I want to tell everyone, but . . ." She read the message
again.

Molly stood up. "Let's put it away somewhere
first, then decide what to do."

Jill nodded. "Okay."

Like two excited pirates feverishly
digging up a long-lost treasure, Jill and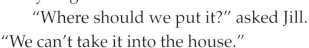
Molly dug the box out of the snow.

"Where should we put it?" asked Jill.
"We can't take it into the house."

"The garage. We'll put it in the storage room
above the garage," said Molly.

Jill took one end of the box and Molly took
the other, and they walked to the corner of the house.
Molly craned her neck around to look up at Ricky's
windows. They were closed. "The coast is clear,"
she said.

Jill made a face. "This box is so heavy my
arms are being pulled out of their sockets," she said.
"There must be lots of great presents inside." Her
carefully bobby-pinned curls hung in bedraggled
clumps.

The girls waddled across the driveway as
quickly as they could. The box pushed against their

stomachs, making it hard to breathe. Step, thump!
Step, thump! Step, thump! They struggled up the
stairs to the room above the garage. Molly pushed
the door open with her back. Once inside, they put
the box down and collapsed like melted snowmen.

"Phew! That was hard," said Jill. She leaned
back against the door.

Molly was sweating under her snow jacket.
Bobbles of snow were frozen on her pajama legs.
Her hands inside her mittens were stiff with cold
and the weight of the box.

Molly and Jill stared at the box.

"So what do you think is in there?" asked Jill.

"Presents, of course."

"Yes, but what?" Jill squatted next to the box.
She smoothed the wet brown wrapping paper.
"Maybe we should open it up, just to be sure nothing
is broken or anything."

"No peeking," said Molly. "That's not fair. Dad
wants everything about this box to be a surprise."

Jill looked sheepish. She sat down again. "But
Dad doesn't know how worried we've been. He
doesn't know what it's been like to wait and wait
and wait for even a letter. He doesn't know how

much we've been hoping for this box."

Molly smiled. "I thought you were being *realistic* about Christmas this year. I thought you said it was childish to hope for surprises."

Jill laughed. "I guess I did. But I guess I really never stopped hoping this box would come. That's why I think we should tell everybody about it right away. They're all hoping, too. It would make them so happy."

"But Dad said to keep it hidden until Christmas Day," Molly answered. "If we tell everyone now, we'll ruin his surprise."

Jill thought a moment. Then she stood up. "Okay. We'd better hide it in the corner, in case someone comes up here."

Molly and Jill pushed the box into the darkest corner of the room. Molly pulled a dusty old blanket over it, then put two broken tennis rackets on top.

"There!" she said as she backed away. "That ought to do it."

The box under the blanket looked like a lumpy brown bear sleeping peacefully in a snug corner. "I sort of don't want to go away and leave it," said Jill. "I'm afraid it's a dream and the box will be gone when we come back."

"I know what you mean," said Molly. "But we'd better go. Everybody will be getting up for breakfast. We can check on the box later."

Jill nudged the box with the toe of her boot. "Good old Dad," she said.

"I *told* you he wouldn't forget," said Molly. "Come on. Let's go. And remember to act as if nothing has happened."

As she followed Jill down the stairs and across the driveway, Molly felt happy—completely, entirely, head-to-toe happy. She and Jill stamped their feet at the back door to make the snow avalanche off their boots. When they went into the kitchen, Mrs. McIntire took one look at them and laughed. "Well, you two look like rosy little elves! Where have you been? Up to the North Pole working on Santa's surprises for all of us?"

Molly felt her face get hot. Mom's joke was too close to the truth. She stooped over to unbuckle her boots. "We were just out—outside," she stammered.

"Playing in the snow," finished Jill.

"So I see," said Mrs. McIntire. She lifted Molly's wet hat off her head with two fingers. "How did you manage to get dirt streaked across your jacket when everything is covered with snow?"

Molly looked down at her jacket. Dust from the old blanket had left a trail across it. She didn't know what to say.

"We were in the garage," said Jill, in a voice as cool and light as a snowflake.

"Looking for the sleds, I'll bet," smiled Mrs. McIntire. "Well, you can go sledding all you like after breakfast. But right now, both of you scoot upstairs

43

and put on dry clothes. Molly, you're still in your pajamas!"

Molly and Jill galloped up the stairs. At the top, Jill yanked Molly into her room and closed the door.

"Phew!" said Molly. "I thought maybe she saw us with the box or something."

"Listen," said Jill. "I think we should tell Mom about the box. Dad probably thought she'd be the one to get it first anyway."

"It *would* be easier if she knew," admitted Molly. "It almost feels like we're lying to her by keeping it a secret."

"That's what I think, too," said Jill. "Besides, she's probably already suspicious. You're terrible at this secret-keeping business. You're acting as if you robbed a bank or something. Mom must suspect you have a secret."

"Well, everybody has secrets at Christmas time," said Molly.

"Yeah, but not as big as this one," said Jill. "Let's tell Mom about the box."

But Molly just couldn't give in. "Telling one person is the same as telling everyone. You can't keep a secret just a little bit. You either keep it completely or give it all away. Dad wants to surprise everyone for Christmas. We have to help him."

Jill crossed her arms. "All right, all right. But how much longer do we have to keep the box hidden?"

Molly thought. "We'll have to wait until everyone goes to sleep on Christmas Eve. Then we'll sneak over and get it and put it under the tree. But until then, absolutely no telling anyone—not Mom, not Brad, *nobody*. Promise?"

"Okay, I promise," said Jill. She grinned. "Now I know how Santa Claus must feel."

Molly grinned, too. "It's not easy to keep Christmas surprises a secret," she said. "But this one is worth it. This will be the best Christmas surprise anyone has ever had."

THE MERRY MCINTIRES

Keeping Dad's secret did not get any easier for Molly. She was jittery all day Saturday. After breakfast, when Brad rushed to the garage to get his sled, Molly planted herself like a guard at the bottom of the stairs to the storage room. Jill rolled her eyes at her and hissed, "Move away!" Molly wouldn't budge. What if Brad went up to the storage room? What if he saw the box? But Brad was interested only in his sled. He didn't even notice Molly.

There was another alarm after lunch when Ricky went to the garage to get a snow shovel. Molly hovered around him so much, Ricky finally gave her a shovel and told her to help out. Molly didn't mind shoveling the driveway. At least she could keep an eye on the garage without looking suspicious that way.

By the end of the day, Molly was exhausted. This secret-keeping business was hard work. And there was still one whole day to get through—one more nerve-wracking day—until she and Jill could reveal the surprise.

The next day was Christmas Eve. Molly was on pins and needles all morning. Luckily, Mom was up in her room until noon, wrapping presents. She couldn't see the garage from there. And Ricky and Brad built a snow fort in the front yard. They spent the morning cheerfully bombarding each other with snowballs.

At last it was time for everyone to get ready to go to church for the Christmas Eve service. As Molly put on her special green velvet Christmas dress, she felt relieved. The secret would be safe while they were all at church.

Molly loved the Christmas Eve service. The church was decorated with red and white poinsettias

and garlands of pine and holly. A dark manger
scene filled the front of the church. Everyone was
given a small white candle to hold. The flame of
Molly's candle flickered and danced as she listened
to the words of the Christmas story:

> "And suddenly there was with the Angel
> a multitude of heavenly hosts praising
> God and saying, 'Glory to God in the
> highest, and on earth, peace, good will
> toward men.'"

Molly knew everyone in her family was
thinking of Dad and hoping this Christmas would

truly bring peace on earth so that he could come home.

Maybe next Christmas Dad will be here with us, thought Molly. She remembered how his deep voice sang out, "Silent night, holy night." Molly looked down the pew. She saw a tear caught like a tiny diamond in the corner of her mother's eye, shining in the light of the candle. Molly bit her lip. *Maybe we should have told her about the box*, she thought. *Maybe then she wouldn't be so sad.*

But when they walked home from church, Mom seemed happy. Their neighbors' calls of "Merry Christmas!" were warm in the snappy cold night.

They had their traditional Christmas Eve supper of scrambled eggs, bacon, hot chocolate, and cinnamon toast before they hung their stockings on the mantle. Mom read *'Twas the Night Before Christmas* just as Dad read it every year. They all knew that the last line of the poem was their signal to go to bed. So everyone stood up and said with Mom, "Merry Christmas to all and to all a good night!" Then they ran up the stairs to their rooms and jumped into bed.

TICK, TOCK, TICK, TOCK, Molly's heart thudded with every tick of the clock. She was waiting, waiting, waiting for it to be midnight. At midnight she and Jill would perform their secret mission. They would put Dad's box under the Christmas tree.

Molly opened her eyes very wide. Her room was solidly dark, filled corner to corner with blackness. She rolled over on her side and looked at her glow-in-the-dark clock for the millionth time. 11:56. Only four minutes to go. She couldn't wait any longer. She sat up. Did her bed always creak so loudly? Slowly, carefully, she stood up and tiptoed to the door. Slowly, carefully, she opened it.

BOOM! A white shape bumped into her. Molly gasped and the white shape giggled. It was Jill. She put her finger over her lips to signal "no talking." Molly put her slippers on her feet, and they both went into the hallway. They felt their way down the stairs in absolute darkness, putting two feet on each step like unsteady babies. Molly didn't even breathe until they got to the kitchen.

Jill headed to the closet to get her jacket. Molly grabbed her arm and whispered, "No! Too noisy!" All of a sudden, she felt sort of wobbly. She moved her hand down Jill's arm and Jill squeezed it. Molly felt better. She opened the back door and went outside.

The cold bit their skin. Quickly they dashed across the driveway, up the stairs, and into the storage room.

"This is kind of scary, isn't it?" Molly whispered.

"Oooh, I think it's fun," said Jill. "It's like a ghost story."

Molly shivered. "Come on. Let's hurry." They carried the box down the icy steps, across the driveway, through the kitchen, and into the living room, then put it under the tree. There were several tempting boxes that had not been there under the tree before. Molly pointed to them. "Santa Claus has been here," she said.

For some reason that made both Jill and Molly burst into giggles. They grabbed pillows from the sofa to muffle their laughter. When they finally quieted down, they crept up the stairs to bed. Jill waved good night outside her door. Molly waved back. *Mission accomplished*, thought Molly. She curled up under the covers, drowsy and happy and very, very relieved.

"MOM! MOM! MOM! MOM!" was the next thing Molly heard. She opened her eyes. The sun was just coming up and her room was rosy. "Mom!" she heard Brad call again as he thundered down the hall. "Merry Christmas! Get up!"

The McIntires had a rule that no one could go downstairs to the Christmas tree until everyone was ready. Brad banged on Jill's door, then Molly's door, then Ricky's door. When they were all gathered at the top of the stairs, Mrs. McIntire smiled and said, "Okay, go ahead!" Everyone stampeded down the stairs.

At the door of the living room, the stampede stopped suddenly. "Hey," said Brad, "what's that big box?"

Ricky rushed past him to the tree. "Mom!" he squeaked. "It's from Dad! Look, it's from Dad!"

Mrs. McIntire's face went white. "From . . . ?" she whispered. She knelt down next to the box and touched the label. She looked up. "It is! It's from your father! But how?" She looked at Jill and Molly. They smiled. Mrs. McIntire sat down on the floor.

"You two!" she laughed. "Why didn't you tell us about the box?"

"Dad said not to," said Molly. "Look." She pointed to Dad's message.

"Keep hidden . . ." Mrs. McIntire read. "Just like your father! Always surprises!" She hugged first Jill, then Molly. Molly could feel her trembling.

"Well, what are we waiting for?" said Ricky. "Let's open it." He tore the brown paper off the box and ripped open the lid.

"Oooh," said Brad. "Look!"

The box was filled with green tissue paper lumps in odd shapes and sizes. Each lump was labeled.

Ricky handed them out. "One for Brad. One for Jill. One for Molly. One for Mom. One for me."

53

Brad opened his bundle in no time. "A canteen," he said contentedly. "And a soldier's hat. I guess Santa asked Dad to get them."

Ricky had a silk scarf made from a genuine parachute—the kind real pilots wore. Jill had a heather-colored skating hat. "*Much* nicer than Dolores's," she said with satisfaction. Mom had buttery-smooth leather gloves. She slid her hands into the gloves and smiled as she pulled out a small white note. She seemed too happy to say anything.

"Oh, look!" cried Molly. Everyone knelt around her as she lifted her gift out of its rustling tissue paper. Molly's gift was a doll—a beautiful doll with dark shiny hair and smiling blue eyes. Molly touched the doll's hair with one finger and traced the curve of her pink cheek. She was dressed in a nurse's uniform and hat like the one Molly had dreamed about. A smart red cape covered her starched dress and tied under her chin. Molly hugged her. This doll would be her friend, her companion in adventures, the secret sharer of all her dreams. And when she played with her, Molly would always remember that Dad had chosen this doll for her. Even though he was far away, he still knew what would make Molly the happiest girl in the world. If only Dad could be there with them to see how happy his surprise had made them all.

"Well," said Mrs. McIntire suddenly. "What time do you think it is?"

"It's exactly 7:03," said Ricky, who never took off his watch.

Mrs. McIntire glanced at the white note in her hand, then put it in her bathrobe pocket. "Let's turn on the radio," she said. "We can listen to the Christmas shows while we open the rest of our presents."

Ricky flicked on the radio. Christmas music filled the room. "Joy to the world!" the singers sang. The music was drowned out with whoops of delight as Brad and Ricky, Jill and Molly opened present after present. Molly was glad to see that not *all* the presents she got were so very practical. Jill gave her a glass ball that filled with snowflakes when she shook it, and Brad gave her a corsage he'd made out of pine cones and red ribbon.

"I'm Captain James McIntire,"
said a familiar voice.

All too soon, all the presents were unwrapped. Molly sat in a sea of crumpled wrapping paper, eating Christmas coffeecake. Brad insisted on drinking his juice out of his canteen. Ricky flung his scarf around his neck and pretended that he was the voice on the radio singing,

"May your days be merry and bright,
And may all your Christmases be white."

Then a scratchy voice on the radio said, "Merry Christmas! We're broadcasting from the USO Christmas party in England, and we have some servicemen here with messages for the folks back home. Here's an eager fellow. What's your name, Captain?"

"I'm Captain James McIntire," said a familiar voice. They all stopped still and looked at the radio. "I'd like to say Merry Christmas to all the merry McIntires—Jill, Ricky, Molly, Brad, and my wife, Helen."

Molly held her doll very tight.

"I miss you all very much. And I hope you have a wonderful Christmas full of happy surprises."

And that was all. Other soldiers

spoke, but Molly didn't hear them. She kept the echo of Dad's voice. She never wanted it to fade. Dad. What he said was still true. There *were* always surprises at Christmas.

LOOKING BACK 1944

A PEEK INTO THE PAST

"Realistic" was the word Jill used to describe Christmas during World War Two. Molly may not have liked it, but that was a pretty accurate word to use. Soldiers were fighting and dying in countries all over the world, and the war was having a very "realistic" effect on Christmas in America.

The war separated families. Almost every family felt the sadness of missing someone in the Armed Forces who was far, far away. Thousands of Americans were fighting. But only a few lucky soldiers got *furloughs*, or permission to go home for short holiday visits with their families.

Most soldiers were in dangerous or uncomfortable places. They were lonely and homesick. When they mailed their Christmas packages, they dreamed of going home, too.

People who stayed back on the home front

Few soldiers went home for Christmas, so letters from their families were more important than ever.

60

were separated from their families, too. Wartime work in factories couldn't stop for Christmas, so celebrations had to be squeezed in to busy schedules.

It was hard for people to go visiting, too. Because of the war, most families were allowed to buy only three gallons of gasoline a week. That meant they could not drive their cars very far. They couldn't drive very fast, either, because the "Victory Speed

A wartime poster and gasoline ration coupons

Limit" was 35 miles per hour. It took a long time to go anywhere at that speed, so many people didn't have enough time to make Christmas visits by car. They didn't travel by bus or train because busses and trains were

filled with soldiers, sailors, and marines on their way to training camps. So, sadly but patriotically, many families were apart at Christmastime.

But Americans fighting on the home front had grown to be strong and clever people. They learned to find

Americans who lived near training camps invited soldiers and sailors to their homes for Christmas.

61

Home-front cooks learned to bake without much sugar or butter.

ways of getting along without things they wanted. For example, families were allowed to buy only one stick of butter a week. Sugar was rationed, too. But home-front cooks made up new recipes for Christmas cookies and treats that used less butter and sugar.

People on the home front used their imaginations on their Christmas trees, too. They couldn't buy new ornaments because factories were making war equipment instead of lights or balls for Christmas trees. They

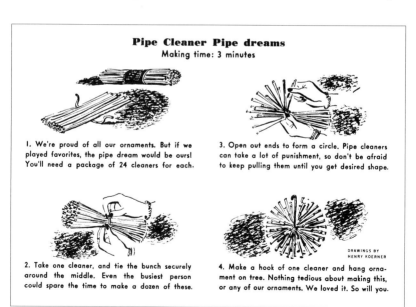

Pipe Cleaner Pipe dreams
Making time: 3 minutes

1. We're proud of all our ornaments. But if we played favorites, the pipe dream would be ours! You'll need a package of 24 cleaners for each.

2. Take one cleaner, and tie the bunch securely around the middle. Even the busiest person could spare the time to make a dozen of these.

3. Open out ends to form a circle. Pipe cleaners can take a lot of punishment, so don't be afraid to keep pulling them until you get desired shape.

DRAWINGS BY
HENRY KOERNER

4. Make a hook of one cleaner and hang ornament on tree. Nothing tedious about making this, or any of our ornaments. We loved it. So will you.

Magazines showed people how to decorate with homemade ornaments.

couldn't buy tinsel because metal was being used for guns, planes, and binoculars. They didn't even have a lot of paper for paper chains because scrap paper was collected and reused as part of the war effort. So most families polished up their old ornaments and thought of new ways to make Christmas merry. Sometimes they decorated their trees with flags or with letters from their relatives who were far away fighting.

During World War Two, factories weren't making many toys. Some things, like bikes, were almost impossible to get until the fighting was over. Most American children knew they would get things they really needed rather than things they dreamed about

Toys from a wartime Sears, Roebuck catalogue

for Christmas. Like Molly, they expected sensible, practical gifts. But as Dad would say, "There are always surprises at Christmas." During World War Two, mothers and fathers tried hard to make Christmas special for their children. The Sears, Roebuck catalogue still had toys children hoped for and dreamed about. Things like model planes and ships were very popular. Letters to Santa Claus still asked for games, puzzles, sleds, paint sets, yo-yos, and, of course, dolls.

Even during the war, American families found reasons to be happy at Christmastime. The holiday gave

A wartime Christmas card

them a chance to stop working and worrying for a little while. They found that the joy of Christmas carols, snowy streets, window displays in stores, and candlelight services at church as well as the friendly, generous spirits of their neighbors could not be dimmed by the war. Perhaps the war made them think about the real meaning of Christmas and listen more carefully to the words from the story of the first Christmas: "On earth, peace, good will toward men."

THE BOOKS ABOUT MOLLY

MEET MOLLY • An American Girl
While her father is fighting in World War Two,
Molly and her brother start their own war at home.

MOLLY LEARNS A LESSON • A School Story
Molly and her friends plan a secret project to help the
war effort, and learn about allies and cooperation.

MOLLY'S SURPRISE • A Christmas Story
Molly makes plans for Christmas surprises,
but she ends up being surprised herself.

HAPPY BIRTHDAY, MOLLY! • A Springtime Story
An English girl comes to stay with Molly,
but she's not what Molly expects!

MOLLY SAVES THE DAY • A Summer Story
At summer camp, Molly has to pretend to be her
friend's enemy and face her own fears, too.

CHANGES FOR MOLLY • A Winter Story
Dad will return from the war any day! Will he arrive in time
to see the "grown-up" Molly perform as Miss Victory?

◆

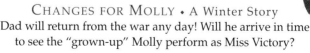

WELCOME TO MOLLY'S WORLD • 1944
American history is lavishly illustrated
with photographs, illustrations, and
excerpts from real girls' letters and diaries.